MW00947045

PRINCESS AND THE CASTLE

By Olinda Gabriele

Published 2019

Printed in the United States of America
Print ISBN: 978-1-7338384-9-8

Canoe Tree Press
4697 Main Street
Manchester, VT 05255
www.CanoeTreePress.com

I grew up in a small poor town called Montagnola in the southern part of Italy. We had no television; therefore, at night my mother would tell us stories to keep us busy. I started telling stories to my children when they were young and I continued to tell them to my grandchildren, they enjoyed the stories.

I want to dedicate this book to my children, grandchildren, and my husband. My family has given me the inspiration to share my imagination.

Olinda Gabriele

Once upon a time there was a man named Jon who lived in a very poor town called Zu Town with his wife Lily. Children in Zu Town had no television or toys.
On a very stormy night, Jon and his wife Lily heard a loud knock on their door.

"Jon, did you hear that?" Lily asked with a very scared voice.

"Yes, Lily," Jon said calmly, "Maybe it's the wind fighting again with the clouds." Jon looked out the door and saw that the wind was very strong, and the clouds with their big fiery red eyes and big arms like gates were keeping the moon from shining. It looked like they were having a wrestling match, and the clouds were winning. Jon quickly shuts the door and goes inside.

As Jon and Lily sat quietly, there was another loud knock on the door; this time it was so loud that it shook the house. Lily and Jon jumped so high that they both hit their heads on the ceiling. "Ouch" they both yelled. As they started to rub their heads, they realized that they now had a flat head just like a pizza.

Jon, still rubbing his pizza head, grabbed a chair and held it for protection while he slowly walked near the door. Jon was a little scared, but he was trying to be very brave for Lily.

Jon opened the door and nervously stepped outside. He looked to the right, then he looked to the left, but nothing was there. "Well, Lily," Jon said with a sigh of relief, "I told you it was the wind and the moon fighting. Let's go back inside."

As they turned to go back inside, to their surprise, they heard something that sounded like a baby crying. Jon scratched his pizza head thinking, "Goodness, I really hit my head pretty hard! Now I hear a baby crying; there are no babies around here." Jon and Lily turned again to go back in the house, but the sound of the baby crying became louder. Lily shouted, "Look Jon! There is a box on our steps, and I think the crying is coming from that box!" Jon slowly walked near the box and carefully opened it. To his surprise there was a baby in the box. The baby was so beautiful; it looked up at Jon and started to giggle. Lily quickly picked up the baby and cuddled it. Attached to the baby's beautiful soft purple blanket was a note that said, "Please take care of this baby, for this is the safest place for her. She will bring you love and happiness."

Jon and Lily looked at each other, still in shock, and said, "Who brought this baby to us? How are we going to feed a baby? We have no extra food or clothes."

Lily, still cuddling this beautiful little baby, turned to Jon with a smile and said "Don't worry, Jon, it will be okay! We shall name her Sofi."

They took the baby into their small house and shut the door.

Many years went by, and Sofi turned out to be a sweet beautiful little girl with long beautiful brown hair and big beautiful blue eyes. She loved to dance and sing, and every day she went outside to practice.

Sofi was also a good helper around the house and did all her chores without being reminded.

One bright sunny day Lily was cleaning her room and noticed that it was time to make new sheets for her bed. She then thought to herself, "I can make a beautiful dress for Sofi with these old sheets and surprise her." She quickly started making the dress. The dress was red and purple, but there was something missing. Lily wanted the dress to flow like a princess, so she found some green grass and sewed it around the hem to make it flow like a princess dress.

One beautiful and sunny day Sofi came in from playing outside, Lily said, "Sofi, I have a surprise for you! You have been a wonderful little girl who always helps mommy and daddy, and we are very proud of you!"

Sofi was so excited that she started jumping up and down and said, "What is it mommy?"

Lily said with excitement, "Close your eyes, and don't peek!"

Lily took Sofi's new dress out from an old box and said, "Open your eyes!"

Sofi opened her eyes and screamed with excitement, "Mommy this is the most beautiful dress that I have ever seen! It's like the dress that I always dreamed about; you're the best mommy!" Sofi took her dress and ran to the kitchen and hugged her father with excitement. She put the dress on and danced for hours just like a princess at a ball.

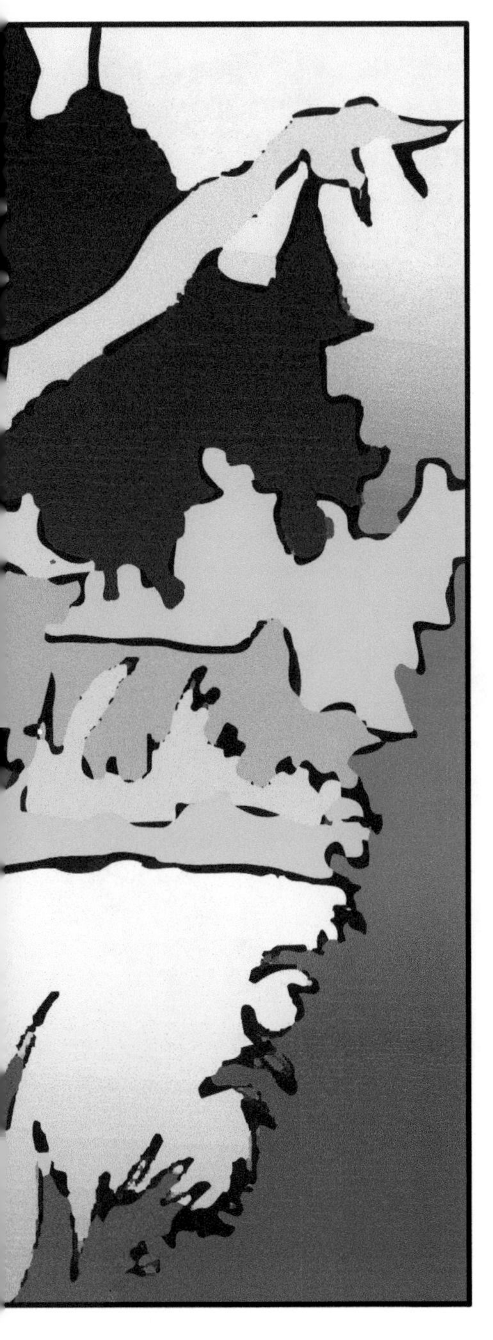

As years went by Sofi was now a big girl. She didn't have any friends to play with, she was always home with her mommy and daddy; making her feel very lonely. The beautiful dress that her mother had made her no longer fit, she was wearing very old clothes. She didn't feel like a princess anymore, making her very sad.

Sofi decided to go and play outside. While she was playing, the sky got very dark and the trees started swinging back and forth making awful sounds. The wind started fighting with the clouds again, the birds were flying backwards, the cats were walking on two legs, and the chickens were hopping like frogs.

Sofi didn't know what was going on and everything around her became so dark that she couldn't see anything. The wind was very strong and the sounds were very scary. Sofi fell to the ground and put her face into her hands wishing very hard for everything to stop.

After a few minutes the wind and all the awful sounds stopped. Sofi slowly stood up from the ground and turned to walk to her house but it wasn't there. "Where is my house? What happened? Mommy, Daddy -- where are you?" But no one answered. Sofi yelled again, "Mommy, Daddy!" but again, no one answered. Sofi started to cry. She cried and cried until she heard someone say, "Stop crying! You are giving me a headache!"

Sofi jumped and said, "Who said that?"

"I did, and you woke me up from my nap," a voice replied. Sofi wiped her tears away looked up to see a purple and green owl on a pink tree with sparkly and shiny leaves. This was the most beautiful tree Sofi had ever seen. "I am sorry," said Sofi, "but I am scared."

"Yeah Yeah," said the owl, "It doesn't mean that you can give me a headache."

"I am really sorry," said Sofi still wiping her tears away. "Can you help me find my family?"

"Just when I thought that I was going to have a quiet day...." the owl sighed. "Okay, let's go!"

The purple and red Owl with Sofi started walking to find Sofi's family. They walked for a very long time and to their surprise, they saw a mouse with a purple hat trying to jump from rock to rock. The mouse stopped and looked at Sofi and the purple and red owl. "Why are you staring at me? Are you making fun of me?" said the mouse in a very angry voice.

"No" said Sofi "I think you're really good at jumping."

"Where are you going?" asked the mouse in a more friendly voice.

Sofi said, "We are looking for my family. There was a big storm, everything got dark, and now I can't find them."

"Can I come and help?" asked the mouse.

"Sure," said Sofi, "what is your name?"

"My name is Jack," said the mouse.

"My name is Sofi, and this is my friend Mr. Owl".

So off went Mr. Owl, Sofi, and Jack.

After walking for a very long time, they heard an awful noise. They stopped and looked around but they couldn't see anything, so they just kept on walking. Jack started jumping up and down yelling, "I see something! I see something!" Sofi and Mr. Owl stopped and looked up, and to their surprise they saw a castle. The castle sparkled like shining stars, with beautiful rainbows and flags around it. They could not believe how beautiful this castle was.

They started running as fast as they could toward the castle. After running for a while, they stopped to rest. "It seems like the castle is moving further away every time we try to get closer; that is so strange." Sofi said.

They looked at each other very confused, but suddenly the awful sounds they had heard before started again and this time the sounds were louder.

"You know it's time for my nap," Mr. Owl said in a very grumpy voice.

"Your nap?" Jack shouted.

"Yes, you know like finding a good branch and going to sleep!"

"Going to sleep?" Jack yelled again, "We need to get to that beautiful castle and find out where this awful sound is coming from. It's driving me crazy!"

As they continued to walk, the castle still seemed to move away. Then a very loud laugh came from the sky. It was so loud that Sofi, Jack, and Mr. Owl had to plug their ears. Jack shouted, "I see something flying in the sky! I think it's an elephant!" Mr. Owl and Sofi giggled, and Jack felt that they were making fun of him again and became very sad.

"Jack, elephants don't fly!" giggled Sofi.

"Look! It's really an elephant," said Mr. Owl, "and someone is sitting on it."

The laugh became louder and suddenly the elephant landed with a giant thud in front of Sofi and Mr. Owl. On the elephant was a witch. Her nose was as big as the elephant's trunk and she had a wart on her nose as big as a soccer ball. "I have never seen anyone so ugly," said Mr. Owl.

The witch looked at Mr. Owl and pointed her finger at him in anger, "I will cast a spell on you."

"No!" yelled Sofi. "He is my friend; leave him alone, why are you so mean?"

The witch put her head down and said, "I have no friends to play with and everyone makes fun of me and calls me ugly."

Again, the terrible sound became louder and louder. "Where is this awful sound coming from?" Sofi asked.

The witch laughed and said, "A long time ago I put a spell on the castle the day the princess was born, for the King was always mean to me."

What kind of spell?" asked Sofi.

"I wished that the King and Queen would never be happy. I tried to cast a spell on their baby princess, I wanted the princess to grow up to be ugly and be sad like me but someone took her away, and that made me so mad. I have been searching for her for a very long time."

All this time Jack was hiding in Sofi's dress pocket for he was really scared of the mean witch.

"You must break the spell," Sofi bravely demanded to the witch.

"I cannot break the spell," said the witch laughing out loud. "The only way the spell can be broken is if the princess returns and enters the castle. She must first climb over that big dark wall, but this will never happen for many have tried and failed," laughed the witch.

"But no one can get near the castle, because the castle keeps moving away." Sofi said in a very sad voice. "You must help us."

"That is not my problem," laughed the witch. "You figure it out! See you later, alligator!" and she flew away laughing.

"Listen everyone," said Sofi "We need to team up and never give up! We must keep on trying." They started walking again and suddenly they heard another strange noise that sounded like a horse. Just like magic, this beautiful white horse with a very handsome man sitting on it stood in front of them. The horse had diamonds all over his tail and was wearing green shoes.

Sofi asked in a shaky voice, "Excuse me, Sir, we hate to bother you, but we need some help. Can you kindly help us?"

"I am very busy," said the man, "for you see, my father, the king, from a far-away land, said I need to find a bride very soon, or he will find one for me. And I don't want him to pick my bride. He has no taste."

"We will help you find a bride if you can help us get close to the castle," said Sofi.

"This castle?" the prince asked in shock.

Mr. Owl wisely said, "Yes, this castle. What, do you have wax in your ears? Honestly, I don't understand some people sometimes."

The prince, a little shocked by the mouse's rude reply, explained "There is a spell on the castle and no one but the princess who was born there can ever break that spell."

"But we must try," pleaded Jack as he slowly climbed out of Sofi's pocket. "Please help us!"

The handsome prince looked at them and saw how sad they all were.

"Okay, let's go. Hop on my horse," said the prince.

They quickly hopped on the horse; they rode and rode for a very long time until they finally arrived near a big wall.

"We must turn around," said Mr. Owl, "for this is the dark wall the witch was talking about."

"No," said Sofi, "we came this far and we need to find a way to get over the wall so that we can get to the castle and find my family."

The owl, still thinking how great a nap would be at this time, thought to himself that if he helped them, he would be able to get back to his tree and take a nap.

"I know we can do it as a team" said Mr. Owl, "But I am super sorry that I cannot fly because I am so tired, and I have no energy, but I do have a plan: we can have someone step on the horse and jump over the wall."

"Good idea," said Jack "I will go first, I am a good jumper."

So Jack got on the horse and tried 100 times to jump over the wall, but he kept falling. Then the prince tried, and he fell right on his back. The only other thing left to do was to help Sofi get over the wall. They all teamed up and helped Sofi onto the horse and pushed her over the wall. As soon as Sofi went over the wall, the sky, the trees and the ground started to shake. Everyone was scared. They did not know what was going on.

The birds started flying straight, the cats started walking on four legs, and the chickens stopped jumping like frogs. Flowers started to grow, and the sun came out with a big smile. Looking up at the sky they saw that the clouds and the moon stopped fighting. The awful sounds stopped and beautiful music started playing.

The black wall disappeared and right in front of them was the beautiful castle. The gate from the castle opened up and the prince, Mr. Owl, and Jack went in.

The castle was so beautiful and sparkly that they could not take their eyes off it, but where was Sofi?

"Sofi, Sofi, where are you?" Everyone started to yell.

They walked in the castle, and there was Sofi in front of a mirror. This mirror was the biggest mirror anyone had ever seen. The mirror started to dance and shake, sparkling lights were spinning around it, and suddenly giant lips with shiny lipstick appeared.

"You have returned home, Princess Dafnie," said the mirror. "You have saved the castle and everyone who has been under the spell. We have been waiting for a very long time."

"Why, what do you mean?" Sofi asked the mirror.

"Many years ago, you were taken away from the castle to be saved from the ugly mean witch. The witch put a spell on this castle, but now you have returned, and you have saved everyone," Said the mirror.

"A princess?" Sofi asked still in shock. "But I live with my parents in Zu Town. I am not a princess -- there must be some mistake!"

"There is no mistake," explained the mirror, "Please come closer and take my hands." Two hands with pink nail polish appeared from behind the mirror and reached for Sofi.

"Don't be afraid," said the mirror, "reach for my hands" Sofi was very scared but she slowly walked near the mirror and touched the hands. Suddenly purple and green lights with stars started spinning around her. When the spinning stopped, Sofi had turned into a beautiful princess with the most beautiful dress that has ever existed. Her hair was shiny and sparkly to match her dress.

Jack, Mr. Owl, and the prince could not believe their eyes that Sofi was the missing princess.
"You are Princess Dafnie!" sighed Mr. Owl.

"Wow! You are so beautiful!" sighed Jack

"You are the most beautiful girl that I have ever seen," said the prince, "Will you go to the ball with me?"

"I must find my mommy and daddy," said princess Dafnie. "But first, I wish to help someone." She turned to the mirror and said, "Will you help me?"

"Anything for you Princess Dafnie," said the mirror with excitement.

"I grew up very lonely and never had any friends to play with," Princess Dafnie humbly stated. "I wish for the mean witch to be happy."

Jack, Mr. Owl and the Prince looked at each other in shock, and the mirror spun around three times in a most confused manner.

"But princess Dafnie," said the mirror, "the witch has always been very mean!"

Princess Dafnie turned and looked at the beautiful mirror with very sad eyes and said, "I know that she has done mean things, but now that I am the Princess, my wish is to change bad things to good things. Please grant my wish."

"As you wish, Princess Dafnie" said the mirror.

As the mirror started to shake, baby birds with red and purple wings started to fly around the mirror playing beautiful drums. Every time the birds hit the drums, rainbows came out and went up to the sky filling it with beautiful rainbows.

Everyone looked up to the sky, and to everyone's surprise, they saw a flying elephant with a pretty girl sitting on it. "Look!" yelled Jack, "It's the witch, and she is smiling." The witch waved to them with a beautiful smile and flew away. Everyone was happy!

The prince put the princess and her friends on his horse and off they went to Zu town.

The princess's mommy and daddy, the queen and king, were so overjoyed to see her. Princess Dafnie helped everyone in Zu town and gave lots of toys and clothes to all the children.

The princess, along with Jon and Lily, the couple who loved and took care of her, moved into the beautiful castle. She gave Jack a super cool trampoline so he could practice his jumps, and she gave Mr. Owl a beautiful tree with a purple bed so he could take his naps. She and the prince had a magical time at the ball.

Soon they married, and everyone lived happily ever after.

THE END